Can You Spot
The Spotty Dog?

For Michelle

A Red Fox Book
Published by Random House Children's Books
20 Vauxhall Bridge Road, London SW1V 2SA

A division of Random House UK Ltd
London Melbourne Sydney Auckland
Johannesburg and agencies throughout the world

Copyright © John Rowe 1996

3 5 7 9 10 8 6 4

First published in Great Britain by Hutchinson Children's Books 1996

Red Fox edition 1998

Printed in Hong Kong

RANDOM HOUSE UK Limited Reg. No. 954009

ISBN 0 09 949751 4

Can You Spot
The Spotty Dog?

John Rowe

RED FOX

Can you spot the spotty dog?

If you can, turn over.

Can you spot the spotty dog
And the little white owl?

If you can, turn over.

Can you spot the spotty dog
And the little white owl
And the jet black cat?

If you can, turn over.

Can you spot the spotty dog

And the little white owl

And the jet black cat

And the tiny grey mouse?

If you can, turn over.

Can you spot the spotty dog

And the little white owl

And the jet black cat

And the tiny grey mouse

And the slippery snake?

If you can, turn over.

Can you spot the spotty dog

And the little white owl

And the jet black cat

And the tiny grey mouse

And the slippery snake

And the furry mole?

If you can, turn over.

Can you spot the spotty dog
And the little white owl
And the jet black cat
And the tiny grey mouse
And the slippery snake
And the furry mole
And the prickly hedgehog?

If you can, turn over.

Can you spot the spotty dog

And the little white owl

And the jet black cat

And the tiny grey mouse

And the slippery snake

And the furry mole

And the prickly hedgehog

And the bright white butterfly?

If you can, turn over.

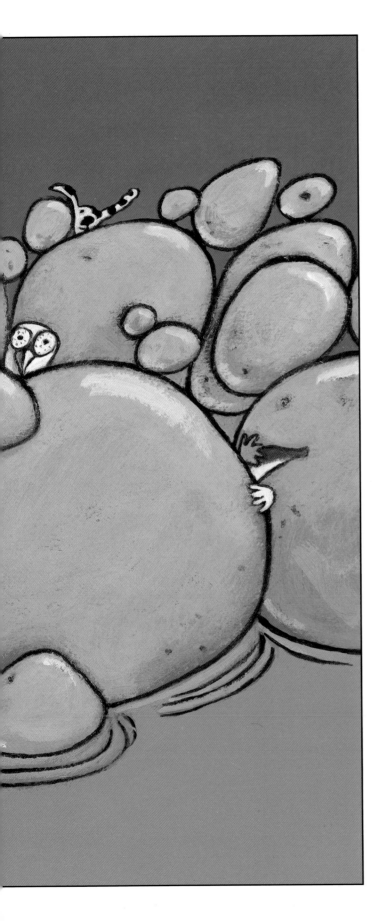

Can you spot the spotty dog

And the little white owl

And the jet black cat

And the tiny grey mouse

And the slippery snake

And the furry mole

And the prickly hedgehog

And the bright white butterfly

And the hungry hippo?

If you can, turn over.

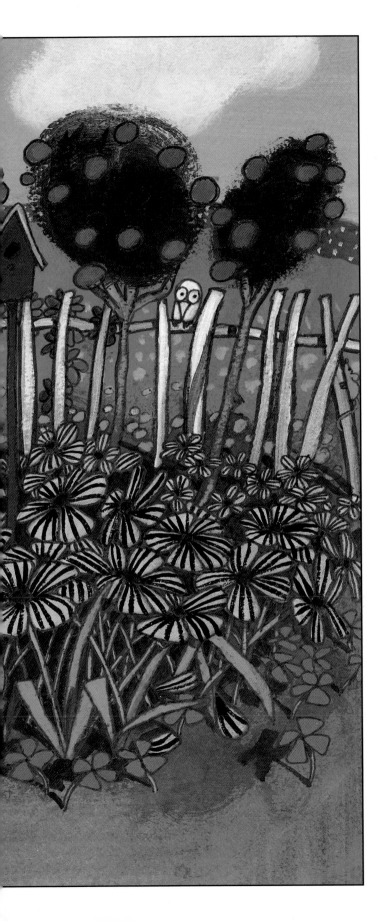

Can you spot the spotty dog

And the little white owl

And the jet black cat

And the tiny grey mouse

And the slippery snake

And the furry mole

And the prickly hedgehog

And the bright white butterfly

And the hungry hippo

And the busy bee?

If you can, turn over.

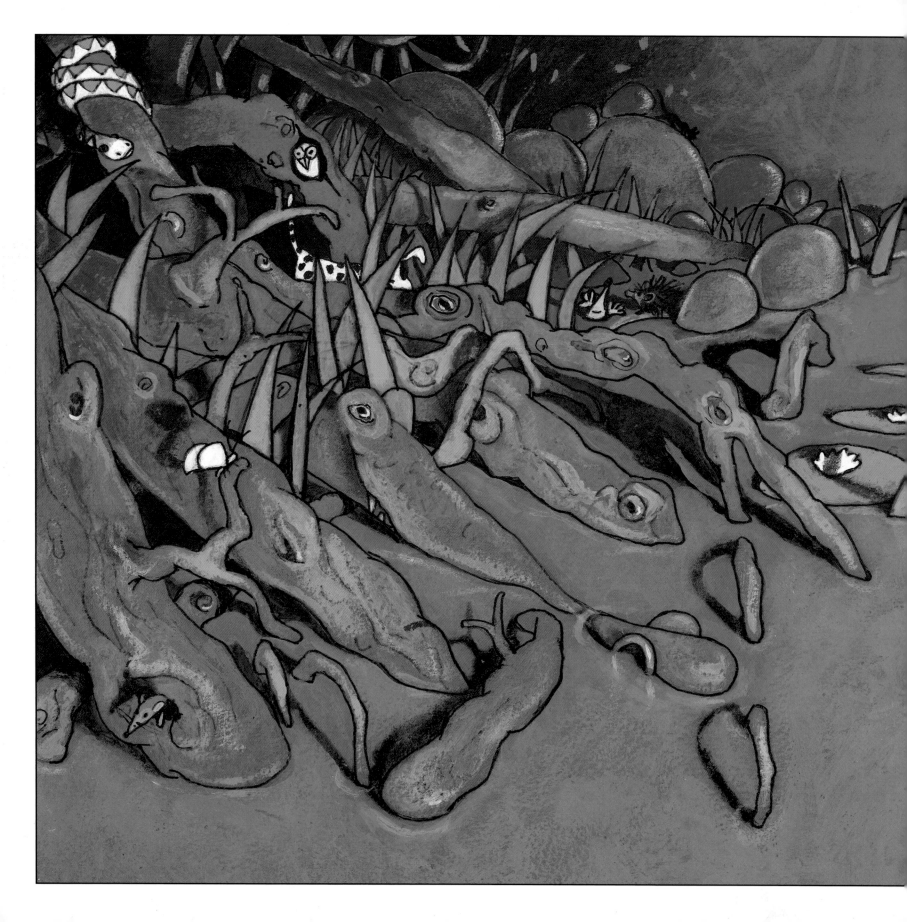

Can you spot the spotty dog

And the little white owl

And the jet black cat

And the tiny grey mouse

And the slippery snake

And the furry mole

And the prickly hedgehog

And the bright white butterfly

And the hungry hippo

And the busy bee

And the crusty croc?

If you can, turn over.

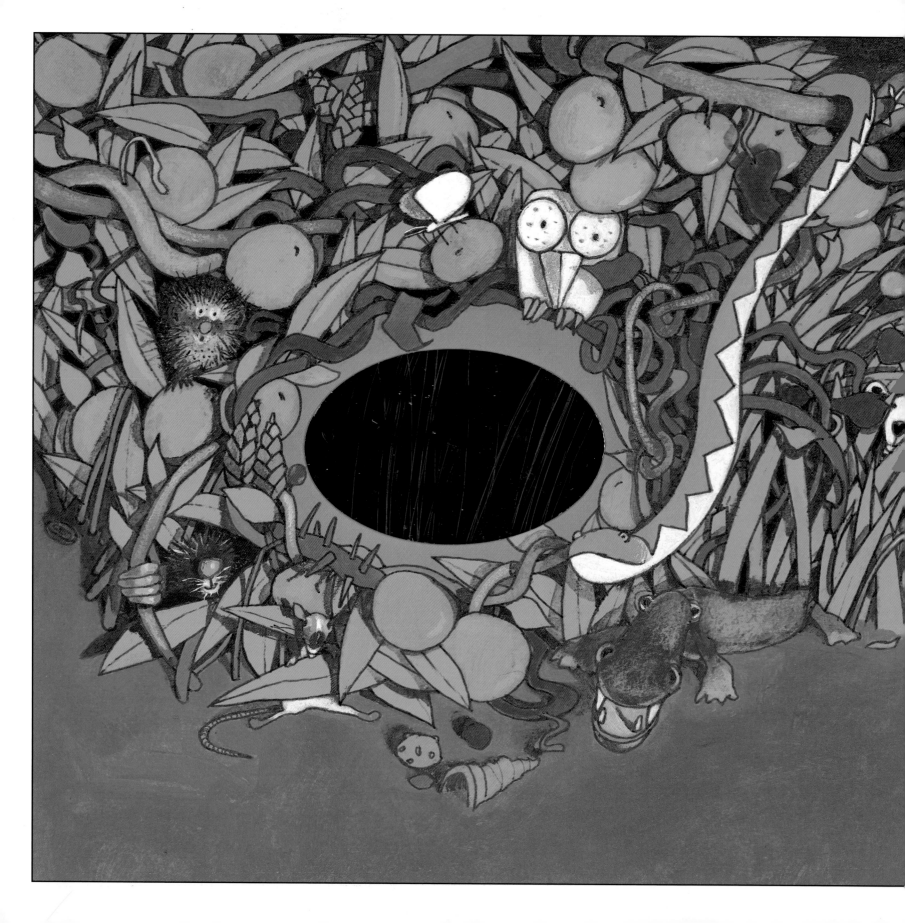

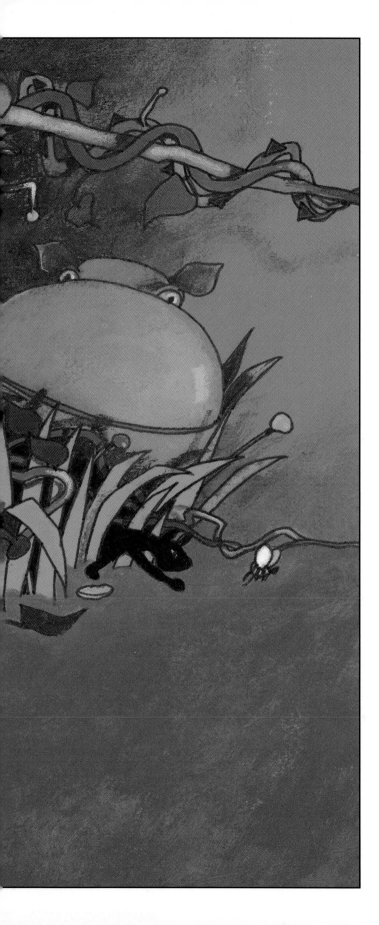

Can you spot the spotty dog

And the little white owl

And the jet black cat

And the tiny grey mouse

And the slippery snake

And the furry mole

And the prickly hedgehog

And the bright white butterfly

And the hungry hippo

And the busy bee

And the crusty croc...

And the cheeky monkey?

Some
bestselling Red Fox
picture books

THE BIG ALFIE AND ANNIE ROSE STORYBOOK
by Shirley Hughes
OLD BEAR
by Jane Hissey
OI! GET OFF OUR TRAIN
by John Burningham
I WANT A CAT
by Tony Ross
NOT NOW, BERNARD
by David McKee
ALL JOIN IN
by Quentin Blake
THE SAND HORSE
by Michael Foreman and Ann Turnbull
BAD BORIS GOES TO SCHOOL
by Susie Jenkin-Pearce
BILBO'S LAST SONG
by J.R.R. Tolkien
WILLY AND HUGH
by Anthony Browne
THE WINTER HEDGEHOG
by Ann and Reg Cartwright
A DARK, DARK TALE
by Ruth Brown
HARRY, THE DIRTY DOG
by Gene Zion and Margaret Bloy Graham
DR XARGLE'S BOOK OF EARTHLETS
by Jeanne Willis and Tony Ross
JAKE
by Deborah King